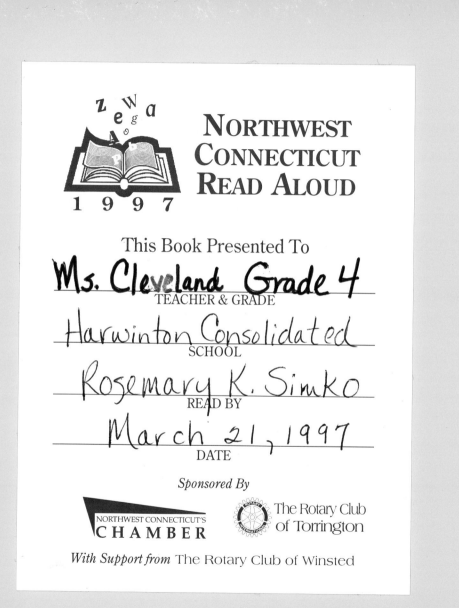

ZEWAga

NORTHWEST CONNECTICUT READ ALOUD

1997

This Book Presented To

Ms. Cleveland Grade 4
TEACHER & GRADE

Harwinton Consolidated
SCHOOL

Rosemary K. Simko
READ BY

March 21, 1997
DATE

Sponsored By

NORTHWEST CONNECTICUT'S **CHAMBER**

The Rotary Club of Torrington

With Support from The Rotary Club of Winsted

The Fish Princess

STORY BY IRENE N. WATTS • ILLUSTRATIONS BY STEVE MENNIE

TUNDRA BOOKS

efore she learned to speak, she sang songs of wind-whipped waves, of gulls crying, of water lapping.

Before she learned to walk, she swam, for she was a child of the sea.

Shells whispered the secrets of the deep to her, and sea foam fastened necklaces of creamy pearls around her throat. She played in the water and was never afraid.

But the villagers were afraid.

They remembered when the calm sea turned wild. They remembered the boat drifting to shore. The moonlight had glinted on the dark waters, and inside that golden circle a fisherman found the baby girl lying in the empty boat, smiling and cooing her strange songs. No one knew who had manned the oars. No one knew from where she had come or to whom she belonged.

The villagers feared the child, for she was not of their kind. They were afraid of what they could not understand. Unheeding of their warning voices, the fisherman carried the baby indoors.

"The sea has sent you to comfort me," he said. "I will be your grandfather, and I shall take care of you." From that day on, she lived with him. She was his only family, and he was hers.

The villagers shunned the fisherman and the girl. As she grew, no children came to take her berry picking; no women braided her hair. On feast days she danced alone. When the villagers told their stories, she sat apart. When she made necklaces of shells, only her reflection in the rock pools, and in her grandfather's eyes, told her she was beautiful.

And every morning and evening, she walked beside the ocean, singing the song she had always known, the song of the sea. And in that song, she sang of her longing for the sea to bring her a friend.

The waves answered her, the birds beckoned, the tides drew her into the water, but she always pulled away from their call and returned to her grandfather.

Their life together was good. The pain of being an outcast was eased, for she had her grandfather to laugh with, to listen to, to teach her and to love her. They ate fish and berries and corn, and were at peace.

Her grandfather taught her how to cast the nets and haul them in and to throw back the fish too small to eat. He showed her how to watch for signs of anger in the sky, and when to wait out the sea's rage in sheltered coves. She listened to his words, but sometimes she felt as if she had always known.

One day, returning from a small sand-silvered bay, they watched the skies grow dark, the waters fierce and black. They reached the village and saw the fish piled high in glittering heaps. Too many to eat, to smoke, to store. Yet still the knives gleamed as the fishermen struck and struck again.

The girl halted her song.

One great deep-sea salmon thrashed about in a net. The girl stood beside him, trembling. She stared at the silver blade poised high. Slowly, slowly the knife was lowered-put aside.

The girl picked up the great Salmon King, returned him to the ocean, and watched him swim away.

The villagers cursed the girl, whispering their fear. "Now we will go hungry. She keeps the fish from us."

The next day and the next and many more were wild and stormy, stormy enough to keep the fishermen home.

The girl's thoughts were only of the salmon she had freed.

At last the sun reappeared. The girl went to wake her grandfather. She found him lying pale and weak.

"Take out the boat," he said. "Today you must go without me."

She rowed to the fishing grounds and sang a song of praise to the fish. As she sang, she searched the horizon and looked deep into the waves, hoping to see the salmon she had saved. He was not there.

That day, the net contained enough. In the evening, she sat beside her grandfather and fed him.

On the second day, when she hauled in her net, she found a circlet of gold among the fish. Her song of thanks carried to the shore.

When night fell, her grandfather said, "It is our time to part. Tomorrow when you reach the bay, light a fire. Put on your crown of gold and sing your song. I will listen one last time and take your words inside me to the other world."

That night, he died. The girl brought her grandfather to the bay and buried him in the sandy cove. She mourned him. Then she waited by the ocean as before.

When the sun rose on the third day, she cast her net and lit a fire. She placed the crown upon her head. Her song was full of sorrow and hope.

When she hauled in the net, she knew, even without looking, what it would contain. The Salmon King said to her, "Draw your knife and cut off my head." She cut. The drops of blood that fell on her hand felt like her own tears.

Again he spoke, "Now, with the tip of your knife, cut the length of my body. Then put me in the fire." She did so. The flames leapt up-orange and blue and silver. From their midst stepped a young man whose eyes were as deep as the rock pools, as dark as the eyes of the Salmon King.

He held out his hand to her. "Princess, of all the fish that swim from the river and stream into the bay, we have waited a long time to find each other. Let us go home. You shall sing your songs forever, and you will never be alone again."

Together they walked into the sea. Before the waters closed around them, the Fish Princess turned to look at the burial mound upon the shore. She called out, "You will always live in my heart."

And in the silence was heard the song of the sea.

© 1996 Irene N. Watts: text
© 1996 Steve Mennie: art

Published in Canada by Tundra Books, Toronto, Ontario M5G 2E9

Published in the United States by Tundra Books of Northern New York, Plattsburgh, N.Y. 12901

Library of Congress Catalog Number: 96-60353

Canadian Cataloguing in Publication Data:

Watts, Irene N., date
    The fish princess

ISBN 0-88776-366-9

    I. Mennie, Steve   II. Title.

PS8595.A873F58   1996   jC813'.54   C96-900247-5
PZ7.W36Fi   1996

The publisher has applied funds from its Canada Council block grant for 1996 toward the editing and production of this book.

Designed by Sari Ginsberg

Printed in Canada

00 99 98 97 96   5 4 3 2 1